THE BATHS
OF ORGASMIA

Also by ESMERALDA LINTNER

FIFI'S EROTIC BOUTIQUE
A Store of Pleasure

LINCOLN MEETS WASHINGTON
An Historical Fantasy

FIFI'S NAUGHTY RHYMES and FAIRY TALES
Make Believe Erotica

FIFI'S NAUGHTY RHYMES and FAIRY TALES
Volumes 2 and 3

TRUMP: THE PRINCE OF FOOLS
A Musical Fantasy

TEDDY, HARRY and DICK
The Presidents Speak

LADY FARTINGHAM
An Historical Tale in
Flatulent Taste

REVEREND STIFFWILLY
A Heavenly Endowment

TWO-TIMING TILLIE
Femme Fatale

THE SHADOW OF FALSE FACE

A GHOUL'S DELIGHT
Full of Fiendish Fun

MONIQUE'S PLEASURE PALACE
Zany & Erotic Fun

THE WACKY WHACKING-OFF WORLD OF SEX
Naughty & Bawdy Antics

THE
BATHS
OF
ORGASMIA

An Ancient
Roman Fantasy

by

ESMERALDA LINTNER

**Contains several illustrations
and numerous photos**

Cover design provided by kdp.amazon.com
Cover photo provided by shutterstock.com

ISBN 9798883934246

First printing March 2024

Printed in the United States of America

Dedicated to the memory of

FRANKIE HOWERD
(1917-1992)

and the gang at
"UP POMPEII!"

The wild tale we all are about to hear takes us back --- way back, that is --- to Ancient Rome. The year is 30 BC. The story is an erotic one, very exotic and full of orgasmic orgasms. Although rather naughty, the story is historical as well. So then, put on your toga and pull it down well, for the opening scene takes place in downtown Rome at the very popular baths of all times known as Orgasmia.

The owner/proprietor of these baths is none other than Longus Dongus. On any given day, we'll find him supervising and overseeing the operations of his baths. The man in question is five feet eight inches tall and has medium jet-black hair. He relishes passing out fresh towels to all his customers. Looking past the throngs of people crowding into the baths, he begins speaking directly to us, the readers of this extraordinary story.

"Welcome to *Roma Caput Mundi*, our glorious capital city," he begins. "If you prefer, you can call us *Urbs Æterna*, the Eternal City." Scratching his head and looking perplexed, he adds, "Hmm..., Sounds all Latin to me. But enough of these crazy Latin vocab lessons already! Y'all can just call this big ol' city Rome. This is the place where the lions roam and feed upon the criminals and non-worshipers of the great Caesar. And boy oh boy, them lions've gotten themselves one big ol' varied menu to choose from!"

Continuing to hand out towels to the bathers, he goes on, "Y'all caught me doin' one of my motherly chores. You've got to have a towel in hand --- and not only in hand, but also around the royal naked tush. Hey, that reminds me: I first got wind of an incident which took place this very afternoon, don't'cha-know. That cat named Cornelius who's a big rancher out this way --- he just happens to own the largest wheat and olive farm in these parts --- was recently caught with his toga down. That alone caused quite a stir among not only the women, but also some of the boys. Both male and female alike noticed that ol' Cornelius had somethin' 'tween his legs the size of an elephant's trunk. That ought t' prove to y'all that they don't call this here place Orgasmia for nuthin'."

Bathers who were paying attention to Longus Dongus's descriptions laughed up a storm as they continued grabbing towels from him. "I heard through the everlovin' grapevine that folks here have lots of orgasmic experiences, shootin' high enough to reach the top of good ol' Mt. Olympus. I'll bet ol' Jupiter's smarted in the eye and that it's knocked him right off his friggin' throne. Somethin' like that might well blind the mighty king of the gods."

Folks come to the baths in order to wash, chitchat

and socialize, and to exercise or to work out so that they can buff out their bodies. "That's an especially big attraction for younger men, y'know," Longus Dongus exclaims. "Girls really go for a guy with hot muscles. Whoo-whee! I've even seen a couple of the older men ogle the younger ones 'cause they're in search of a servant and a lover as well. If you're figurin' t' socialize, this is the place. You never know who you're gonna hook up with! Cupid can strike with his erotic arrow at any given moment."

Fanning himself from getting so excited, our intrepid bath proprietor says, "Why, just the other day two people met here. Their names are Pomona and Titus, and their first meeting occurred under my very roof. 'She's the apple of my eye,' the lad exclaimed. That's a real knee slapper, for Pomona's name means 'apple,' don't-cha-know. That horny little brat added, 'I'd like t' pick me some apples off'n her tree anytime. Them fruits are nice 'n ripe, all the better t' munch on.'"

Clearing his throat and smirking, Longus Dongus resumes his description. "Enough 'bout those two. As I said before, some folks also come here to relax and refresh themselves. We've got a nice café and an adjacent library. Our thirsty patrons can take a swig of wine or beer as well as the ever popular *posca* (that devilish mixture of vinegar and water in quantities which make it drinkable and refreshing). The servers there also lay out dishes of dates, olives, flatbread, various kinds of cheese, and so on --- you know, a little *nosh*, as those wily Hebrews would say. While nibbling, our patrons catch up with the latest news and views written on the scrolls."

Blinking and reflecting on this pleasant vision, Longus Dongus continues, "If a guest gets fed up with just lounging and takin' it too easy, he can walk around the lush gardens we've got here, soaking up all the wonders which Terra, the Roman goddess of nature, provides us. Speaking of nature, it often takes its course," the bath proprietor adds with a grin. "*Inter*course, that is. The steam room's notorious for that kind o' thing. Boy oh boy, it sure is hot in there. There's a whole lot o' rompin', stompin', raunchy, raucous activity as the steam rises to the marble walls. It sure is a great place to come and spend the time o' day. You know the old sayin', don't cha? '*Every day, and in every way, one gets better.*' This area of the baths consists of several rooms. Once you get rid o' your threads in the *apo-*

dyterium, you head into the hot room. We call it the caldarium. From there you get your behind into the washing room. By this time, the sweat oughta be pouring off'n you. You'll be a sweathog, for sure! With all the hot bodies gathered there, one thing leads to another, and you've got yourself a mess o' unbridled unspeakable, unmentionable, wild releases. In other words, folks are gettin' turned on! Raunchy sexual activities of unbelievable magnitude always take place."

Longus Dongus works himself into a frenzy, wiping his brow and heaving a great sigh. "Man oh man, is Cupid ever workin' overtime here at the baths!"

II

Besides being the owner of this fun place of fanciful frivolity, Longus Dongus has an extracurricular activity. "I betcha didn't know that I happen to be a musician and poet *par excellence*," he quips. "In fact, I'm known as the greatest in all downtown Rome. Not to be braggin' on myself, but I'm the top act in town. Lemme give y'all a few samples. Take my flute (*aulos*) here," he says, waving the instrument for all to see. "If y'all look really close, you'll see that it's made o' metal. Boy, there's no *metal*ing around with this instrument."

Tapping the finger holes, the bath proprietor goes on, "It has the regulation number of finger holes which may be alluring to some of y'all. So then, grab yourselves a li'l ol' folding stool, and *away we go!*"

Rubbing his chin, Longus Dongus adds, "Hmm…, methinks I stole that line from some famous celebrity or comic who'll probably be livin' in the future. I just dunno."

Longus begins playing his soothing melodies. In between sets, he pauses to recite one of his poems. One of them goes like this:

> *"Come one, come all,*
> *Where you'll have a grand ball,*

Washin', heatin', relaxin',
Exercisin' that body of yours away.
You'll leave these here baths
Sayin' they're just grand,
And that I, Longus Dongus,
Am the greatest, mighty fine,
This guy's A-OK.
Longus Dongus is my name,
And when you all come here,
You'll have the biggest relief
Of all the ding-dong places
Whence you came.
Come, orgasm, climax if'n ya like,
If you didn't have one or reach it,
Then you can always take a hike.
The Baths of Orgasmia's the
Place to be.
Just the two of us,
Or maybe three?
Let's head on over to the hot tub,
Shall we?"

Longus casts his flute aside and takes a quick bow. "Here's a juicy musical interlude for ya, folks. It's another little rhymee-whymee one fer y'all." He launches into the second song called simply, "Love":

"Love is in the air,
Love is in the air,
Why not take a dip

Into Orgasmia's Baths
If'n you dare?
Nuthin' beats goin' bare
In the steam room
Under the bright, hot sun of the gods.
Y'all better watch yourselves
Or that fairy'll slap ya
Right in your love bun.
Love is fine,
Love is fun,
When you're here in Orgasmia
Havin' your orgasmic fun."

Longus Dongus finishes his racy song and takes a deep bow. "Wowee, folks, y'all almost got an eye full there! My toga just went up over my li'l ol' head." Chuckling, he adds, "Y'all can see why they don't call me Longus Dongus for nuthin'."

III

There are many stories one could tell about this place. "Some would burst your toga wide open," Longus Dongus proclaims. "Take, for example, the *palaestra* --- in other words, the courtyard. It's an open-air garden where you can exercise, do work outs and tone up that hot body of yours." Looking down at his belly and clearing his throat, our proprietor chuckles, "Mine? A hot body?! Y'all have got to be joshin' me. Your contact lenses sure must be out of focus."

Walking through the *palaestra*, Longus Dongus explains, "Take two of our lads who often get into athletic competitions: Gaius and Marcus. Talk about hot bods! Just the sight of one of them would make a guy jealous and a young maiden drool all over herself. I needn't mention what it would do to some of the boys either. When Gaius gets going with those exercises of his, look out. Them muscles o' his pop and bulge out like nobody's business. He's well defined all over, including his dinger-donger as well. Gifted and virile in more than one way, of course. He sure as hell pours on the charm."

Catching his own breath, the bath owner exclaims, "Yes indeed. That guy surely has the appearance of a young buck --- playful and wild. He's got the most revved-up dickiest prick in all of Rome." Pausing for effect, Longus Dongus continues, "Now that other guy, Marcus, is someone entirely different. That hunk is more into exhibitionism. When he works out, he lifts weights in a manner for everyone far and wide to catch a glimpse. He's even known to grab a nearby marble statue or two, giving the poor unsuspecting work of art a few good pumps. If I did something like that, I'd end up in the hospital with a double, even triple hernia. That'd really put me out of commission. Marcus shows off his muscle-born power even more when groups of attractive ladies stroll by."

Giggling, proprietor Dongus adds, "Just between you and me, it's all goin' to that rascal's head, especially the one down there 'tween his hairy legs. That darn Marcus just relishes being the center of attention. He isn't shy about raising his toga to show interested parties how long and lively things are down there. I have half a mind to summon the guard to arrest him for nudity, even indecent exposure if he decides to go all the way."

Longus Dongus rubs his chin and ponders, "Aw, why stop 'im? His exhibitionism may draw more people to these baths. I cannot permit the public to be denied the pleasure of enjoying themselves over this. It would be a real wild release of the fun-filled, playful squirts of their mighty erections. With him on display, it'd be like a hot, steamy explosion of vol-

canic lava. Boy oh boy, just talkin' 'bout this kind o' stuff turns me on!"

Longus Dongus sees some statues and other proud Roman decorations. "On a completely different subject," he interjects, "I must point out these majestic golden marble statues of all the powerful gods and goddesses we worship." Bowing before one of the statues, he adds, "Here is Minerva, full of knowledge and wisdom. Ain't she a beaut?"

Glancing at the sky, our bath proprietor remarks, "Excuse me, O Blessed and Sacred Minerva, I'm not tryin' t' get fresh with ya or anything like that. In case all you readers need a refresher course in Roman history, Minerva's name translates as 'knowledge.' Y'all can get a heap of guidance from her. Let's all bow and curtsey, whatever y'all's pleasure, out of respect to her."

Inadvertently, Longus Dongus bends one knee and slightly dips. "Oops," he cries, "I just did a curtsey in front of the goddess. Must be my feminine side rearin' its ugly head again."

Approaching another of the statues, our guide and proprietor announces proudly, "Over here we have the goddess of agriculture, Ceres. With her magical touch and blessing, she makes our crops grow and our fields abundant, causing us to prosper."

Longus Dongus walks over to another massive statue, one depicting a horseman. "And here we have an equestrian statue of Marcus Aurelius, a great warrior. He rides on his mighty steed, ready for battle. He numbers among other Roman celebrities such as Augustus Prima

Porta and several more depicted in these statues. Kind o' proud lookin', ain't they? Them and all these other cats of whom we have statues."

Strolling farther down a corridor, Longus Dongus declares, "We also have a number of priceless treasures and artifacts. For example, get a gander of these huge urns. And feast your eyes on these marvelous sarcophagi! We got us a whole mess o' ancient scrolls from them Greeks, too."

Our guide/proprietor leads us out of the corridor into an open space. "Lastly, you'll notice the composition of the rooms here. All are walled in marble and decorated with fine paintings. And get a load of these mosaic-covered floors and the big ol' sculptures over there! We Romans have that special eye for artistry. We all have talented, skillful hands. We're a class act, ain't we? The talent you see on display here don't grow on trees! Aside from all that, this joint's a plant-lover's dream; it's all here for you and everybody else to enjoy while y'all 're here." Longus Dongus recites a little poem he made up:

> *Do your thing*
> *While you have*
> *An orgasmic fling!*

"Golly gee," Longus Dongus quips, "I'm a friggin' poet and don't know it!"

IV

Rubbing his chin and thinking, Longus Dongus muses, "Why don't I enjoy a nice cleansing session in the steam room? Like I always say, if ya can't beat 'em, join 'em. When in Rome, do as the Roman's do, ain't that right?"

Our proprietor removes his toga and proceeds into the steam chamber. "Hey, hey," he cries, "if it ain't one o' my regulars." Saluting with two fingers, he shouts, "Howdy there, Juno baby. How're tricks?" Juno is a stunning woman with shoulder-length hair, a svelte figure, and smooth alabaster skin with hints of a peachy tone. She acknowledges Longus Dongus and smiles.

"Hello there," she says, "sorry for bein' away so long. I've been busy around the house, mostly putterin' in the new garden. I've been growin' a whole mess o' fresh veggies, you see."

His eyes twinkling, Longus Dongus inquires, "And how's your love life been?"

Juno grins and her cheeks blush slightly. "Thanks for askin'," she replies. "I've been datin' this new guy. His name's Julius. He works as a defense attorney and gives a helpin' hand to our poorer, most vulnerable citizens. He loves challengin' the authori-

ties who've made it a naggin' habit of throwin' folks to the lions. His appeals have even reached the throne of the Great Caesar."

A mischievous grin crosses the bath proprietor's face. "I'll just bet those giant felines can sniff out a 'client' a mile away!"

Juno laughs and casts a glance at Longus Dongus's crotch. Seductively staring at him, she puts in, "You can say that again, Long-Donger baby!"

Our intrepid bath proprietor smiles and responds, "Why, my dear, I simply had no idea that you cared." Juno places her soft hand upon his lap. "Wowee," Longus Dongus quips, "between the hot steam and your sweet little gestures, you're makin' this donger o' mine longer than ever."

Juno's eyes grow bigger. "I can see that, big boy," she purrs. "That thing's reachin' clear up to Mount Olympus."

Longus Dongus squirms and says, "I feel like a mighty volcano, waitin' to erupt at any moment."

Smiling, Juno answers, "I'll bet you say that to all the girls." Seconds later, a respectable citizen comes strolling into the steam room. Longus Dongus acknowledges the man as he enters.

"Good day to you, sir," he begins. He casts his glance on the well-known orator, philosopher, statesman and lawyer, the great Cicero. "I trust you will enjoy your time here in the baths."

"And good day to you, esteemed Longus," Cicero responds. "There's nothin' like gettin' hot and steamy t' brighten my day. This joint's tops for relaxin' and clearin' my mind, y'know. I get ideas left and right for some o' my upcoming speeches."

Longus Dongus smiles knowingly. "Indeedee-dydee-do, Cicero ol' pal," he chuckles. "Bet you'll be philosophizin' in no time. I always look forward to hearin' one o' your sizzlin' hot speeches. And to think: most o' your ideas spurt from the steam in this here room deep in the heart of Orgasmia."

"Bingo," Cicero retorts. "That steam o' yours has given me some great ideas."

Blushing slightly, Longus Dongus chirps, "Aw, shucks. Thanks, ol' buddy. How kind o' you. I've always held forth that there ain't nuthin' in this world like the orgasmic inspiration which we find solely here in Orgasmia."

Cicero laughs heartily and notices the young maiden sitting next to the proprietor. Mumbling to himself, he says, "I reckon that young damsel ought t' be able t' help me overcome some of the writer's block I've got in completin' this new speech o' mine. That dame can make me rise in more than one way: all the way from thew top o' my head down to the tip o' my 'little mind,' 'mint stalk' or, if you wish, our Latin word for the darn thing, *mentula*."

Overhearing everything the man mumbles, Juno scolds him. "Now, now, you naughty boy, behave yourself. Watch yourself, Buster Brown, especially that darn 'mint stalk' o' yours. Behave already." Thinking for a second, she adds, "To be honest, I wouldn't half mind takin' a little taste o' something like that next time."

Cicero formulates a broad plan with her. "Well, my dear, we can start you off slowly with the mint stalk, eventually workin' you up to the *mentula*, babe." This comment makes Juno blush a deep shade of crimson.

"Golly, Cicero," she shoots back, "Looks like I can't take you anywhere. You and I better get our butts over to the *frigidarium*, Pops."

"No need to walk," Cicero replies gallantly. "Allow me to carry you in my arms over there, sweet thing." Longus Dongus smirks as he takes in the dialogue between the two. He rolls his eyes.

"Well, it looks like the youngins are at it again. One track minds --- Orgasmian ones, that is!"

V

Longus Dongus peers over his shoulder and notices a pair of young boys in the company of two older gentlemen. "Well, tear my toga t' shreds, Cupid," he murmurs to himself, "if it ain't them *exolet* kids. At any rate, that's the word we Romans use to describe what I have no doubt future generations are goin' t' describe as an 'escort.' I recognize them scamps 'cause they've hung 'round here before. Their names are Cassius and Albus."

Focusing on one of the two men, our proprietor continues, "One o' them old guys is none other than Brutus the Trojan, the powerfully strong one, the founder and first king of Britain, as legend would have it. I'm sure between him and one o' them lads, a raucous good time will be had. Methinks Cassius has a hankerin' t' be with him. That youngster's into bondage and discipline like nobody's business. Them cheeks o' his'll be redder than a beet before he knows it."

Holding that vision on his brain for a moment, Longus Dongus exclaims, "And look who Albus, that mere snip of a *pueri*, has hangin' on him like glue: none other than Apollo, the warrior. That ol' guy presides over a school of archery. I can hardly wait to see if Albus'll stiffen his bow!"

Rubbing his hands together in glee, Longus Dongus muses, "I hope that quartet won't leave too much of a mess for me t' clean up afterward. When some of these whippersnappers get goin', plenty of seed is spilled all over the place. I end up havin' t' clean sperm trails left on the floors and walls o' the bath. Why they can't take a li'l more care and clean up after themselves beats me. They ought t' invest in some heavy-duty condoms and lay in a good supply of 'em. The condoms we produce in Rome are made from animal bladders and the muscles from slain enemies, y'know. No artificial color or flavorin's. The leadin' brand's called ORGASMUS. Sort of a play on words with Orgasmia, but a bit more ridiculous."

Harking back to times past, our aging proprietor says, "Ah, I fondly recall bein' in the flower of my own youth. It's times like these which inspire me t' come up with a poem." Directing his attention to Cassius and Albus before they depart, Longus Dongus adds, "This one's for you, boys." The duo casts their glances on the bath owner, and he says, "Here we go! I call this little work o' mine 'The Springs of Youth':

When I was young and in my prime,
I could do it almost all the time.
That metula o' mine was all
ready and up,
It was as playful as a little wild pup.
Youth had me springin' where juices flow,
Cupid blessed me and let me take big squirts, don't-
cha-know..."

Cassius and Albus applaud and the former shouts, "That poem was a gasser, Longer Donger."

Albus quickly puts in, "Though yours ain't no way as big as ours."

Crestfallen, Longus Dongus murmurs, "Gadzooks, don't them runts have an ounce of shame? That unique Orgasmia touch must be goin' t' their heads. And I mean the 'little minds' they have there down yonder."

VII

"Boy, there sure are a lot of interestin' folks makin' their way to these Baths of Orgasmia," Longus Dongus proclaims. "I feel like takin' a refreshin' dip in the pool myself. Let's see here: I can do a little jump right in."

After diving in and the initial splash, Longus Dongus adds, "There ain't nuthin' like this for relaxation. I'm proud o' myself, too, 'cause I can do the doggy paddle, side stroke as well as back stroke. Gettin' an eyeful o' all these bathin' beauties ain't half bad either."

Longus Dongus directs his focus to one of the patrons. "Speakin' o' beauties, just look what we've got over yonder: none other than Aurelia, the gilded golden one herself."

The beautiful Aurelia is clad in a bathing costume fashioned from golden thread with golden coverings for her ample bosoms. "Hmm," Longus Dongus mumbles, lapsing into the Latin terms for what his eyes behold, "what a juicy *pectus mammae*. Just look at those beauties and how they glisten in the sun. It makes her look like she's got a heap big pair o' golden boobs. When that ol' sun hits "em, it practic'ly blinds me. Just imagine bein' blinded by a pair o' knockers!"

Our proprietor watches the beautiful damsel swim gracefully on the water's surface. The other male attendees keep watchful eyes on her, too. "Hmmpf," Longus Dongus sniffs, "just take a gander of them other men in here. They're eyeing that beauty like a pack o' wolves, a bunch o' horny hedgehogs. Hey, she's swimmin' over here my way. I guess some of us guys have all the luck, right?"

Splashing closer, she greets the proprietor warmly. "Well, hi there, Longus dear, how're ya gettin' on today? You're up and longer than ever."

Longus replies nervously, "I always like to rise to the occasion."

Giggling, Aurelia responds, "There's nuthin' like a nice relaxin' swim to keep you up, alive and active."

As she says these words, an eruptive rumbling of volcanic proportions occurs within the water surrounding Longus Dongus. "Oh, how true, Aurelia," it cries. "How true indeed!"

"Oh, my oh my," the bath proprietor shouts, "are all you gods listening to me? Here comes that pompous old windbag, known for disrupting everybody's day. It makes a fella's long dong shrink down into a slip of a thing. She turns ya off instead of turnin' you on! It's Claudia!"

The woman who Longus Dongus and the rest of Rome despises is tall, stocky, with a round, pudgy face, and beady eyes that squint. Thinking to himself, Longus Dongus mumbles, "She's the haughtiest prima donna, that one! I'd better zip my lip and keep my comments to myself. After all, she's one of the wives of Pontius Pilate. I ain't got a hankerin' t' be executed, Roman style.  I don't wanna be hangin' on some ol' tree. I'd better watch what I say or they'll leave me with no tongue to talk with."

Longus Dongus paints a smile on his face and greets Claudia effusively. "Good day, ma'am, are you having a nice day? You look ravishin', by the way."

Frowning, Claudia snaps back, "What the hell's so good about it? The weather's miserable, and my mascara's dripping from my face in this hellish heat. And *ravishing*, you say? Me? Cut it out, will ya? I'll have none of your vulgar comments. I know all about your nasty reputation, especially with all the other dames in town."

Longus Dongus grins and replies, "You forgot 'bout the boys, my dear." This forces the frowning woman to crack ever so slight a smile.

"What the hell? Are you swinging both ways now, Longus you rat? If you don't watch your step, someone'll give you a swift kick in that big, long dong of yours. Pow, right in the *testes*, baby!" Getting right in Longus Dongus's face, she adds, "Putting it bluntly, big boy, your friggin' balls! In case you've forgotten, my hubby's Pilate, the governor of Judaea, so cool it, buster. I've come here to take a fresh, cool dip in the pool."

Claudia departs, making her way to the changing rooms. The proprietor mutters, "Great holy gods above! That ol' broad must be havin' her monthlies." Scratching his head and wondering, he adds, "And at her age, no less! She's a bitch on wheels." Opening his eyes and smiling brightly, our proprietor/poet says in a sing-song manner, "The bitch is pitching a bitch! That's gonna be the lyrics of my latest and greatest song."

Within a few minutes, Claudia returns. She parades around, showing how beautiful she looks in her new bathing outfit. Longus Dongus takes a quick glance at her. Rolling his eyes in disbelief, he mutters, "My great gods, what sort of monstrosity does she have on this time? Golden lining of beads around her breasts with shiny, glittering, feathery frills decorating the skirt bottom. How gaudy-awful it looks! She really thinks she's the cat's meow. Just the sight of her is enough to stop a charging chariot any day of the week."

Claudia slowly takes a seat at the side of the pool. Cringing with displeasure, she withdraws her feet. "Great god Jupiter," she cries, "the water is too *futo* cold! Do I need to translate that word for you which also has four letters and begins with 'f'? This water's getting my dainty little tootsies all frosty and freezy."

Longus listens to her complaint and thinks, "Maybe I should light a fire under that sassy, sorry *posterius* of hers." The bath proprietor responds, "A thousand regrets, ma'am. I ain't got no control over this here water. Maybe the sun'll warm ya up a bit."

Claudia snidely replies, "Jeesh! No wonder it's so hard to get any good help these days!"

She dives in, causing the pool water to shake and bringing up huge currents splashing around. Longus observes, "That broad looks more like a whale swimmin' under there. They oughta call her, 'Claudia the Great Roman Whale." Shaking his head in disbelief, he adds, "It takes all kinds. I guess that's why Rome's known for being big and great. There are lots of different kinds of folks here. Regrettably, I get some weirdos here on occasion, but it's all in a day's work --- goes with the territory, one might say. I am, after all, providing a vital, much needed service to this great city."

VIII

"Well, well," our distinguished bath owner exclaims, "look who it is! None other than our Great Caesar."

The emperor appears rather young, possibly mid-twenties. He has a special pillow, carried by a boy servant, to place lovingly wherever he cares to sit down. Smiling, Caesar gives the boy a firm whack on his buns, a pinch and a little finger-fiddling between his legs. "Oh, hi there, Longus baby," the Emperor says, "nice t' see ya here today."

Bowing and smiling graciously, Longus gushes, "It's an honor to have you with us."

Caesar grins. "Thanks ever so much, dear Longus. As you know, I'm here to enjoy your precious waters as well as to carouse and debauch in the hot room with a couple of these luscious boy servants of mine." Sitting down and snapping his finger, a boy wearing a golden toga holds a grape between his teeth. Caesar maneuvers his head strategically to pluck the fruit from the boy's mouth, smacking his lips with delight.

"Ah," Caesar brags, "this is an Emperor's life, taking sweet nectar from a hot young lad." Caesar accompanies his host as Longus Dongus leads him to the steam room. Boy servants tug at Caesar's pillow, vying with one another to grab it. Caesar sees this display and decides to firmly spank the rump of any boy who might get out of hand.

"Reserve a room especially for me and my boys, Longus," commands Caesar. He follows this with a proclamation: "This day shall henceforth be known as Orgasmia Day."

Clapping his hands, the boy servants turn up bearing large quantities of food, wine in abundance and all sorts of delicacies. Caesar orders the boys to remove his robe, while he chooses to remove their togas himself. "Let us celebrate Orgasmia Day without restraint. Show your emperor what you two youngsters have got. Dance and play for me and with me! The orgasmic powers of Cupid shall spring forth in jubilation!"

Caesar and the boys romp until the setting of the blazing orange Roman sun. Longus Dongus passes by to check on the Emperor, sneaking a peek in the room without anyone knowing. Murmuring low enough for no one to hear, he thinks, "I've seen and heard lots of things before, but never something like this! I wonder: d'ya think stuff like this might make Rome fall one day?"

While Caesar and his boy servants frolic around

and enjoy their day of playful fun, Longus Dongus makes plans to compose a special musical poem for his beloved Emperor. "I sure hope he'll be pleased by the thing and that it ain't gonna shoo him away. I don't wanna end up singin' to a pack o' lions, y'know."

As Caesar winds up his orgasmic celebrations, he parades around the baths, taking the grand tour and checking out every nook and cranny of the establishment. The proprietor turns to him and asks, "Is there anything I can do for you, my great majestic Emperor?"

Caesar perks up and replies, "Oh, I'm just surveying these wonderful baths you have here. In fact, I personally may ask my Senate to introduce legislation which will provide monthly support for this worthy institution."

Bowled over by his emperor's generosity, Longus Dongus applauds the idea and blurts out, "Great Caesar's ghost! How grateful I am to you, Your Magnificence. I shall bow and thank you many times over." Thinking twice, he adds, "You'll forgive me for the erroneous reference to you, my beloved Emperor. I see without a shadow of a doubt that you're still alive and kickin'."

Giggling, Caesar slaps Longus Dongus on the back and quips, "*No problemo*! Everybody's out to get me all the time, so it doesn't faze me in the least. I've gone through at least a dozen food and wine tasters. Unfortunately, none of them live long enough to let me know if the stuff they eat and drink is good enough."

Longus Dongus dips his head in reverence to the Emperor and exclaims, "I have devised a poem in musical form to honor Your Brilliance, O Great Caesar."

This causes Caesar to smile from ear to ear. "I'd be tickled pink to hear it, dear Longus." The Emperor claps loudly, the signal for his servant boys to prepare a place for him to sit comfortably, not neglecting to slap a bum or two while they go about this task. Longus Dongus bows low before Caesar and launches into his rhyme and melody:

"Here's to Our Leader,
The greatest Caesar of them all!
He's here with us and his boys
All having a great orgasmic ball.
He's so majestic, great leader is he.

Let's raise our voices and glasses to him,
Shall we?
He's got great wisdom, that I've heard,
And they do tell,
This great Caesar of ours is
Really swell.
So then, celebrate, relax, swim in
Great Orgasmia's pool,
I guess he will because
He's certainly no fool.
Caesar, Caesar, hail Caesar,
We hail you, Caesar!
The great leader and guide to us all.
Without you
Rome would surely fall.

Overcome with emotion and wiping away a tiny tear from his cheek, Caesar rises from his place and begins clapping fiercely and shouting, "Bravo! Bravo!" Speaking directly to Longus the poet, Caesar cries, "I shall take you up on the pool part." He gives his orders for the boys to swim with him under one condition: they must be bare-assed naked. Upon giving the command, the group jumps into the pool as Caesar engages in a bit of fiddling and fondling as an extra added attraction.

Longus Dongus watches the lively scene and remarks to no one in particular, "I'm overjoyed that Caesar is having a good time as his normal self!"

IX

Longus Dongus decides to head over to the *frigidarium*, popularly known as the cooling room. Sitting there and relaxing is Felix (the happy, lucky one, according to the Latin translation). He feels happy due to his good fortune. He owns his own business downtown: an adult novelty shop.

Longus greets his customer. "Hey man," he cries, "how's it goin'? How are things goin' with that naughty sex shoppe of yours?"

Felix has red hair, very white skin, and pink, bulging eyes which look like he'd been struck by lightning. "I feel happy and lucky today," he replies, smiling and staring at Longus Dongus with big goo-goo eyes. "I'm such a lucky son-of-a-gun 'cause my store's drawing huge crowds. Even some of Rome's most prominent figures mosey on in: senators, scholars, teachers of the law, military leaders, and even our beloved Caesar once made a surprise appearance. You'd be shocked to learn what they're like, too. My leather whips and rubber-spiked codpieces are both big hits. My penis-shaped cobra snakes sell like hot cakes. Just recently, I added a double-headed model! Generals and military leaders simply love having a ball with them, biting and poking one another. Young servants, male and female alike and she-males, all have a heyday."

Longus bursts into laughter, with Felix not far behind him also cracking up. "I just love the cooling room here," the customer says. "Sometimes, if I stay in this thing too long, I freeze my nuts off. Yesiree, Longus baby, these gonads o' mine were fixin' t' freeze in this contraption." Felix's nonstop laughter is music to Longus's ears.

Longus puts in, "Take care, my dear friend. The last thing you want to do is end up like a popsicle. Y'know, those frozen things they've put off inventin' for the next nineteen centuries." Waving as Felix departs, he adds, "Catch ya later, babe."

Our proprietor goes about checking the   premises

to ensure that everyone gets the best service possible. He comes upon the area reserved for the library. His customers can take it easy and read the latest scrolls for news. He spots Julius, whose name in Latin translates as "youthful" or "bright". And the lad is just that: handsome and very fit. Longus notices him with his nose buried deep in one of the scrolls.

"Ah ha," Longus cries, "I see you are studyin'."

Looking up and blinking as he strokes a downy beard, Julius responds, "Righty-o, man. I've been getting into some of the latest financial news. I enjoy analyzing different businesses, especially in cases where Caesar imposes new taxes. I can sit here for hours, reading the opinions of scholars and philosophers. It's always interestin' what they say about life and what it all means."

Impressed, Longus responds, "You're a chip off the ol' scholarly block. How whippin' smart you are, boy!"

Julius grins and exclaims, "My fondest wish is to release some of my scholarly orgasms in this place, too."

"Ho ho," Longus shoots back, "I see that scholarly brain's done gone t' yer head, child. In case you ain't the wiser 'bout it, I'm referrin' t' that long, thick scroll y'all got 'tween yer legs, sonny."

Rolling his eyes, Julius snaps, "Golly, Longus, you sure do have one helluva one-track mind. If you ask me, there's nothing more enjoyable than getting off those first few splashes."

Longus reflects wistfully, and a faint smile crosses his face. "Oh, it's just like the springs of youth," he tells the lad.

Within moments, in walks Rome's greatest philosophical mind, Lucius Annaeus Seneca the Younger, not to be confused with the chap of the same name except with "the Older" tacked onto it! He is a statesman of this Stoic Era, never exhibiting his feelings openly. He belongs to the school of philosophers bearing that name. Longus rushes to the jowly man and reaches for his hand.

"What an honor it is to see you here today, Your Grace," the bath proprietor gushes enthusiastically. "I see you've come to pore over some of our scrolls in order to fertilize the brain y'all got."

Characteristically unemotional, Lucius replies slowly and cautiously, "It is a privilege to be here. I have come to broaden my spectrum on the philosophy of life."

Julius perks up, cocking his ear in Lucius's direction and becoming interested in what the distinguished man has to say. "Pray tell, O Great Lucius," he pleads, "what are some of your observations?"

"Well, life is one big dream," the stoic man begins. "We are pretenders of that dream. Life is unreal and full of uncertainties. Take nothing at face value in dealing with life. One must stop and analyze the world around you, arriving at your own conclusions."

Longus Dongus smirks. "Sounds like a bunch o' *cacas* t' me," he quips.

Taken aback, Julius retorts, "As in shit, my good man?"

Showing no emotion, Lucius steps in to respond. "That brings me to the next level of my philosophy: the stage where life itself becomes *cacas* as well."

Longus shakes his head and mumbles, "Great gods, this guy's got dung on his brain. Don't he ever quit? I s'ppose that's why some o' these varmints come up with smart-ass ideas." Turning to the philosopher and the boy, he interrupts, "Say, I got me here a li'l ol' poem I penned especially for an occasion like this'n." Both clam up and direct their attention to the bath proprietor, eager to hear his viewpoint. Clearing his throat, he begins:

"Life is wonderful,
Life is grand.
There's nothin' like
Life's helpin' hand.
Life is full o' problems;
Boy, can things go wrong!
Sometimes life can hit ya
Right in yer big long dong!
('That's if ya got one,' he slips in)
Life is here and now,
And who knows 'bout the
Afterlife, anyhow?
Celebrate your life
And cut the bad things out
With yer knife.
Life, life, here's t' life!
Shout and sing
For we'll be flyin'
On the gods' mighty wings."

Julius and Lucius are greatly moved by Longus's brilliant, insightful poem. "Those are some deep thoughts, daddy-o," Julius cries.

Stone-faced, Lucius puts in, "Very well said. Keep up the good work, and someday you shall become a great philosopher yourself, Longus."

Puffing out his chest, the proprietor/poet/future philosopher brags, "Wowee! I'm one great teacher of men! I'll surely go down in the annals of Roman history. I can see my name now, flashing in big letters illuminated by torches: LONGUS DONGUS, THE BIGGEST DANG DONGUS OF ALL TIME!"

Julius snickers, "Don't you mean you'll be the biggest prickhead to all the anuses in Roman history?!"

Lucius stares blankly at Julius, adding, "Now, now. Behave yourself. Our elders deserve respect. With age comes wisdom, you see."

X

Longus Dongus proudly surveys his glorious Orgasmia Baths. As he walks along, he gives a few strokes here, puts on a bit of polish there (especially the statues of the great Roman gods) and makes several nips and tucks in general. Amid this flurry of activity, Cornelius the Potter strolls in. Carrying a recently finished vase (appropriately called *amphora*) made of red glaze, he eyes the busy bath proprietor.

Cornelius is a man in his forties who sports an impressive goatee. Longus is taken by surprise as he spots the distinguished potter. And he can barely keep from staring at the newly created vase. Smiling, he approaches the man and cries, "How good it is to see you, my friend. You haven't visited us for a while, as I recollect." Pointing to the vase, he adds, "I'm crazy about the figures you have depicted on this lovely new vase. Wowee, if'n that ain't a heapin' helpin' o' some hot action goin' on."

Smiling naughtily, Cornelius eyes Longus with a look of seduction which crosses his face. "Well," he quips as his eyes bulge with lust, "when I think of Orgasmia, wild sex orgies immediately come to mind. Lots of nasty, forbidden sexual acts and all that sort of thing." Drool runs down Cornelius's chin as he tries to get the words out. He exhibits all the signs of a hopelessly turned-on young man.

He holds the vase closer for Longus to inspect for himself. "As you can see, there are several scenes from places around your baths. The depictions on the vase make it obvious that sexual relations have taken place."

Cornelius's goo-goo eyes bulge uncontrollably now, bigger and more brightly than ever. Longus Dongus steps in to offer his sage observation: "Man oh man, Cornelius ol' pal, you've got my place down to the longest of the dongers."

Grinning seductively, Cornelius quips, "I made sure of the authenticity of this place, even down to the last set of cock and balls. You'll no doubt note how finely detailed the women's breasts are, too. And those nipples go without saying, of course, along with the bushiest of vaginas --- the hidden cave, shall we say."

Longus bursts out laughing. Slapping the potter on the back, he puts in, "I see that you have the senses of an oversexed mind, my dear Cornelius."

Snickering, Cornelius retorts, "The better to see with my painting how it's going to look in the end, Longus baby."

Taking delivery of the brilliant creation, Longus exclaims, "I'll put this masterpiece in a prominent place where everybody can see and admire it. You'll get plenty of exposure, believe you me!"

"You've got that straight, Longus buddy. Why, I got wind through the grapevine that Caesar himself is interested in some of my pottery."

"No doubt," Longus puts in, "our fearless leader has good taste."

Cornelius is pleased with his visit and shakes the proprietor's hand warmly prior to departing on his merry way. Longus Dongus continues with his usual chores: sweeping up and checking the clear quality of the waters. Shaking his head in disbelief, he discovers a few healthy and very undesirable deposits of doggy doo floating by. He employs a specially designed bronze pooper-scooper to remove them.

Within a short time, Longus is distracted by some whistling and singing. Skipping in is Rome's most effeminate and famous painter. "I'd know that skippity-doo-dah, happy-go-lucky music meister anywhere," Longus muses. "That's none other than Aurelius himself, live and in livin' color, baby."

Aurelius wears a grey smock and wields a huge

collection of brushes and other artistic paraphernalia. Flailing his hands and mincing around wildly, the flamboyant artist screeches in a high-pitched voice, "Ooooh, darling Longus, and how is that luscious long dong of yours doing?"

Flinching and suppressing an obvious giggle, the proprietor reluctantly answers, "If you must know, dearie, it's still hangin' in there, don't-cha-know."

Aurelius grins shamelessly and squeals, "Oh, indeed, lover. I can see it's the biggest and longest ever."

Grinning, the proprietor quips, "You might say it's my pride and joy, kiddo. I suppose you've tripped in here today to check on your paintings which adorn some of the walls of these rooms, huh? I noticed in my rounds that a few of 'em need a tad of touchin' up. Please make certain to do a good job, sweetheart. Your work's the tops, and you're one talented little thing, you! Them paintin's o' yourn really stick out."

Aurelius blushes and responds, "Ooooh, I simply adore something when it sticks out, y'know."

"Yeah," Longus shoots back, "in more ways than one, I'll wager."

Aurelius makes tracks to the steam room, his all-time favorite part of the baths. "My heart goes all aflutter because of all the steamy action in that joint," he gushes. "It revvs up my spirit and revitalizes me for all this touch-up work."

Nodding, Longus Dongus chirps, "Well, whatever turns you and that friggin' touch-up brush o' yours on, baby."

Aurelius wags a disapproving finger. "Naughty, naughty boy," he hisses.

Feigning surprise, Longus asks incredulously, "At age forty?!?" I reckon y'all been sniffin' too much o' that high-powered paint o' yours!"

XI

Longus Dongus takes a break from his managerial chores. Mulling over many concerns of the day, he goes into meditative thoughts. "Boy, has this day ever been busy! So many people to look after and keep track of. I wonder who's gonna show up next? One o' the gods, maybe?"

The sky breaks forth with a huge rumbling, accompanied by a few flashes of lightning. Glancing at the heavens, Longus says, "Just pullin' y'all's legs, my mighty gods." Within an hour's time, two senators walk into the baths: Gaius Tiberias, a consul to the Senate, and Decimus Brutus, a consul designate. Longus approaches the two distinguished gentlemen.

Placing his arms across his breast and bowing low before them in the deepest showing of respect, he greets the two well-known senators. "It is indeed an honor and a pleasure to see you here today," he exclaims.

Gaius, the older of the two, being in his mid-sixties with grisly gray and white hair and wielding an overweight, pudgy body, responds, "Thanks loads, Longus. It's been way too long, y'know. I've been busy with all the legislation the Emperor throws our way plus the endless debates from those windbags in the Senate. Both it as well as they are giving me a pain in the ass. I'm getting too old for that sort of donkey dung -- more like horseshit, if you ask me. Believe me, they're  experts at delivering loads of the stuff. They're just full of it."

Senate Designate Decimus Brutus is much younger, scarcely in his twenties. He is youthful, cheerful, and he has a humorous, joking manner about him. He looks askance at Gaius and blurts out, "Aw, don't be such an old stick-in-the-mud, man. You're always so damn crotchety and *flatus* (the young man inserts the juicy Latin term for "fart"). Enjoy your damn self, for goodness' sake, and relax. That's why we agreed to come here to Orgasmia."

Snidely, Gaius remarks, "For my part, I haven't had a good orgasm in months."

Waving away the senior consul's travail, Decimus quips, "Well maybe --- just *maybe*! --- you'll hit a lucky streak and find a partner you can romp around with here."

Screwing up his shriveled face, he retorts, "I can't get it up anymore, hard as I try, you young rapscallion." Decimus breaks out in laughter and smiles at the older man.

"Hey, come on," he urges, "let's you and me search for some hot, steamy fun. Even you might find someone nice to play around with."

Pain courses through Gaius's body at the sound of such words. "Ouch," he cries, "you're making my arthritis act up again, you whippersnapper. But I guess it's preferable to sitting around in that ghastly debating room and listening to the senators drone on. You might have a bright idea after all, youngster. Perhaps I should start with the steam room. That ought to do me some good. It will soothe my creaky bones."

Decimus pats the older man on the back by way of encouragement. "Come, my friend, let us proceed at once."

Smiling ever so thinly, Gaius opines, "I guess there's nothing like an enthusiastic young person to put one in a good mood. After all, the old saying does ring true: 'with age comes wisdom.' In this case, however, the tables are turned. I hasten to say that 'with youth comes youthful ideas.'" Both he and Decimus hold one another's hands as they head over through the gardens to the steam room.

The senators enjoy their relaxing time in the warm steam room. Even the elder, Gaius, comments, "This steamy place is great for my aching bones."

Decimus, the younger of the two, is amazed how less grouchy his companion becomes. Slapping the elder on the back, the young man chirps, "How great it is to see you loosen up a bit, old man, unlike your normal crotchety self." Decimus then suggests they cool off in the *frigidarium*. Gaius goes along with the idea.

"To be honest," he sighs, "I do need a little cooling off after all this steam. I don't want to end up a roasted wild boar."

Laughing, Decimus responds, "Just get a move on, you old codger, before I have to light a match under those everlovin' *nates* o' yours."

Gaius wags a disapproving finger. "You'd better not even try, you naughty boy," he warns. Slowly upon departing from the *frigidarium*, it is plain to see that the elder lapses into his fretting, complaining self as prior to his visit. "Oh, mighty Jupiter," he cries, "my friggin' joints are acting up again." Snapping violently at Decimus, he shouts, "It was your bright idea to bring me into the hot and then the cold rooms in this accursed place. My bones are killing me again."

Decimus tries his best to calm his senatorial colleague. "Cool it, man," he says softly, realizing the irony of his words, "what you need is a nice, cool dip in that pool over there."

Shaking his head, Gaius vehemently refuses. "Thanks for nothing, squirt," he hisses. "Those last two schemes of yours got me feeling enough pain already."

Decimus dips two feet into the inviting pool and beckons to Gaius. "Hey, don't be such a spoiled sport. C'mon, jump in. You and I know that I just love your companionship, you old fart." With that, Decimus stands and gives Gaius a gentle shove into the pool. "Oops, upsy-daisy," the younger man quips as he leaps into the pool. "Hey there," he calls in a playful manner as he approaches the elder man, reaching toward his chest and rubbing vigorously.

"Hmm," purrs Decimus, "I just love older men, especially ones with hairy chests." Looking down into the wavy impressions caused by the swirling water, he adds, "I also see that you are rising to the occasion, my dear friend. You wouldn't happen to care for a little *orias sexus,* would you?"

Forgetting the pain coursing through his body and breaking into a big smile, Gaius quips, "You don't have to show off your Latin knowledge to me, boy. Just get to the point. A blow job or some head --- that's what you're talking about, huh?"

Without bothering to answer, Decimus dives under the water and begins performing fellatio on the stunned man. "Wow," Gaius thinks, "I can see he's an expert at excelling in those extracurricular activities of Senate life." He punctuated his thoughts with several pleasurable moans.

Longus Dongus is alerted to the volume of Gaius's audible reaction and rushes over to check out what all the commotion is about. Laughing out loud, he muses, "Oh well, it looks like boys will be boys."

Gaius gives Decimus a few playful pats on his buttocks as they skip off. Longus eyes the two and exclaims, "Well, well. It looks as if Cupid has struck again!"

EPILOGUE

"Well now, my friends, what a busy and eventful day this has been! I have two senators who have discovered how much they love one another, and even our great Caesar put in an appearance, can you imagine! You cannot get any better than that, can you, now?"

Grabbing some of the paraphernalia he uses in his rounds, our intrepid bath owner adds, "But enough of my chitchat with you already! I must get back to my never-ending list of chores. Please don't forget: if you're ever in downtown Rome, look me up. The unforgettable, never-to-be-duplicated-anywhere Baths of Orgasmia. You know the old saying: 'Do as the Romans do.' You won't regret it, y'know."

Longus Dongus flashes a "V" sign with his index and middle fingers and slowly fades from view.

F I N I S

ESMERALDA LINTNER is a Huntington, West Virginia-based author and poet who has self-published two dozen or more books on various topics.

For more information please visit

esmeraldalintner.net

Made in the USA
Columbia, SC
04 October 2024

42927800R00035